Mr. Reez's Sneezes

by Curtis Parkinson
art by Sami Suomalainen

Annick Press

Toronto + New York + Vancouver

Mr. Reez was a quiet little man who lived in a quiet little apartment. He was content with his quiet life, reading his books, walking his quiet little dog, and petting his quiet little cat. But sometimes he would put down his book and sigh, "Nothing exciting ever happens to me."

Then one day ...

he was sprinkling pepper on his salad and a breeze from the window swirled the pepper up his nose.

"AAH ... AAH ..."

he gasped, his head back.

The dog and the cat scrambled to get out of the way.

"AAH ... AAH ..."

he gasped again, inhaling more pepper, some dust from the street, pollen from the trees, paint fumes, cat hairs, dog hairs ... and one stray gnat.

"AAH ... AAH ..."

The dishes rattled, the pictures shook, the neighbours covered their ears.

There was one more

" AAH ... AAH .."
Then,

"AAHHCCCCCCCHOOOOOOOOOOOOOOOOOooooooo!"

It was a mammoth sneeze, a gargantuan sneeze, a Guinness Book of World Records sneeze!

It was such a sneeze, it blew Mr. Reez backwards out of his chair! Right out the window!

He sailed across the lawn, past the painter and the gardener.

He narrowly missed a bus,
which slammed on its brakes ...

... and shot out of sight!

The dog barked and barked and the cat tore up and down the drapes, while the neighbours leaned out of their windows to see where the quiet little man from 3C had gone.

He was now flying across the country at the speed of sound. Reports of a flying saucer poured in from excited citizens. The air force sent up a pursuit plane, but it got tangled up in the sneeze, and the pilot had to eject and parachute to earth.

"It was definitely an alien," he reported, "with a weird weapon that stalled my engines."

"Keep it top secret," the generals ordered, "we don't want the people to panic!"

Meanwhile, Mr. Reez was enjoying the view of the mountains and deserts and great cities — until he hit an air pocket and plunged towards the ground.

But the sneeze soon caught him up again, and he sailed along above the treetops.

He soared over a baseball stadium just as the batter socked a high fly ball. It landed in Mr. Reez's outstretched hands.

The crowd roared as the ball disappeared in the distance.

"Zounds!" the announcer exclaimed. "The longest home run in history!"

Mr. Reez sped on, over a church where a wedding was taking place, just missing the steeple and setting the bells ringing by themselves.

"It's a miracle!" the wedding guests cried.

In the excitement that followed, the minister married the wrong couple — a homeless man, who had been sleeping in the church, and the bride's mother, a wealthy widow. However, they decided to make the best of it, and everyone showered them with confetti as they left for their honeymoon.

By then, Mr. Reez was streaking over a tropical rain forest.

"Hi matey, watch where you're going!" the macaws screeched.

Mr. Reez was so startled, he dropped the baseball ...

... which fell into the gaping mouth of an alligator just about to gobble up the eggs in a pelican's nest.

"Aye Caramba!!" the alligator cried. "This egg tastes terrible." And he left in a hurry, much to the relief of the pelicans.

Meanwhile, Mr. Reez thought he would go on forever until, suddenly, a hot–air balloon loomed in front of him. He bounced off the balloon and fell into the basket below.

"Buenos dias," the two balloonists said, and offered to share their lunch with him. A hot tamale had a sprinkling of pepper on it and

"Aaaaah, Aaaaah ..."
Mr. Reez began.

"Aaaaah ..."

He shot out of the balloon backwards. "Adios," said the balloonists.

But this sneeze was much better behaved than the first one. It shoved him straight back home at the speed of sound, and then it left. Mr. Reez tumbled through the window and somersaulted onto the sofa, while the dog barked and barked and the cat tore up and down the drapes.

And the neighbours, when they saw he was back, all leaned out of their windows and shouted ...

"GESUNDHEIT!"

The next day, Mr. Reez threw out all the pepper. Then he settled down to his quiet life once more, quite content to have nothing exciting ever happen to him again.

At least for now.

Annick Press Ltd.

We acknowledge the support of the Canada Council for the Arts for our publishing program.
We also thank the Ontario Arts Council.

THE CANADA COUNCIL | LE CONSEIL DES ARTS
FOR THE ARTS | DU CANADA
SINCE 1957 | DEPUIS 1957

Cataloguing in Publication Data
Parkinson, Curtis
Mr. Reez's sneezes

ISBN 1-55037-557-1 (bound) ISBN 1-55037-556-3 (pbk.)

I. Suomalainen, Sami. II. Title.

PS8581.A76234M5 1999   jC813'.54   C98-931957-1
PZ7.P23918Mr 1999

The art in this book was rendered in watercolours.
The text was typeset in Smile.

Distributed in Canada by:
Firefly Books Ltd.
3680 Victoria Park Avenue
Willowdale, ON
M2H 3K1

Published in the U.S.A. by Annick Press (U.S.) Ltd.
Distributed in the U.S.A. by:
Firefly Books (U.S.) Inc.
P.O. Box 1338
Ellicott Station
Buffalo, NY 14205

Printed and bound in Canada by
Friesens, Altona, Manitoba.